HOW TO DRIVE YOUR FAMILY CRAZY... ON HALLOWEEN

Other Scholastic titles by Dean Marney:

Pet-rified

The Valentine That Ate My Teacher

You, Me, and Gracie Makes Three

HOW TO DRIVE YOUR FAMILY CRAZY!!! ON HALLOWEEN

DEAN MARNEY

AN
APPLE
PAPERBACK

SCHOLASTIC INC.

New York   Toronto   London   Auckland   Sydney
Mexico City   New Delhi   Hong Kong

For Susan

ISBN 0-439-14706-9

12 11 10 9 8 7 6 5   1 2 3 4/0

Printed in the U.S.A.   40

First Scholastic printing, September 1994
First printing, revised edition, October 1999

1

Trick or treat. This is a story about my idiot boogerhead brother and a very weird Halloween. My brother's name is Booger except when my parents or teachers are around. Then his name is Booker, but trust me, either way he's still Booger.

It all started when he decided he was going to dress up like one of those singing raisins for Halloween. He's now in the fourth grade and he's totally weird.

"You are so stupid," I said. "Do you know what you will look like? Do you know what people will say about you?"

"I don't care what other people say and I don't give a care what you think," he said.

"You better," I said, "because you're going to look like a giant booger, which if you ask me, you already are, so you don't even need a costume."

"Mom!" he screamed.

Can I help it if I was only trying to help? Can

I help it if I was born into this family? Was it my decision?

How can it be my fault? He drives me crazy. My mother is always on his side. She thinks he never does anything wrong and I'm always in trouble.

"You little creep," I said.

"Mom!" he screamed again.

My mother didn't even bother to come into the room. She didn't even ask what was wrong. She obviously likes him best and doesn't even care about me.

"Elizabeth!" she yelled from the living room. Elizabeth is my name when I'm in trouble. When I'm not, I'm usually called Lizzie.

I'm called Lizzie and I'm normal looking and my parents like my little brother the best. I've got long hair and a moustache. No, I don't, I'm kidding. I do have long hair and I'm normal looking.

I'm not tall and I'm not short. I'm not weird looking. I'm just normal, which is fine with me.

"Elizabeth, whatever you're doing, please stop. Please do not say another word. Please, get away from your brother right now. Please."

I tried to explain. I started to tell her that I was actually being nice. I was just trying to save him from making a complete fool of himself, but would she listen? Oh, no.

She said, "Elizabeth, I don't want to hear it. I just want it to stop. Please stop now. Do you understand or do we have to move on to threats?"

"Fine," I said, "it's all my fault. It's always my fault. There's always something wrong with me."

My mother said. "Let's not overdramatize it, Lizzie. Just stop."

I went to my bedroom.

I thought, That's what you get for being nice. Let him be a stupid big booger. If anyone says anything, I'll pretend I don't know him. I'll pretend like I've never heard of him. I'll pretend I don't have a little stupid idiot boogerhead brother.

Good thing I'm excellent at pretending.

I calmed down.

Forget about Booger, I thought.

Then I remembered what he did yesterday. We were both standing in the kitchen. I was getting disgusted because he was chewing with his mouth wide-open. I could see his tonsils. He was smacking his lips, too. He had a ton of food all over his face.

I said very nicely, "Would you eat somewhere else? You're making me sick."

He yelled for Mom who was in the living room.

"Mom," he said, "Lizzie is bugging me again."

"Elizabeth?" she yelled at me.

"What?" I yelled back.

"Quit," she said.

Booger stuck his tongue out at me with food on it.

"If Mom wasn't home," I said, "I'd pop you one."

3

"Oh yeah?" he said. Then he clapped his hands to make a slapping sound and yelled, "Mom, Lizzie is hitting me."

"I am not," I said, "he's lying."

"I heard it clear out here in the living room, Lizzie. It's time for you to go to your room."

I barged into the living room.

"Mom, he's lying," I pleaded.

"We're not discussing it," she said, "go to your room."

"But — " I said.

"But nothing," said my mom, "or would you like to be grounded for a week?"

"It's unfair," I said, "he's lying and you believe him."

"I'm not discussing it," she said. "I have better things to do than listen to you two fight."

I could see Booger in the kitchen laughing. He still had food all over his face.

Well, I had to forget about Booger and the fact that my parents like him best. I knew I'd get even some day. Right then, I had more important things to think about.

I hadn't decided what I was going to be for Halloween. I knew I wasn't going to be a raisin for sure. I thought I wanted to be something pretty for a change. I'd dressed up as scary things every year. I thought pretty would be good for a change, like a princess or something.

I was sitting there, in my room. I was sitting

4

there just thinking about Halloween. I was sitting there on my bed with the ugly green bedspread with peanut butter smeared on it from the peanut butter crackers I ate on it last night. I was sitting there and I could feel someone staring at me and I froze.

You know how that feels. You get the shivers that run up your spine and across your scalp. You immediately stop breathing and you can't move. You're a statue.

I was afraid to turn around and look, in case it was true, in case someone was there. I also had to look. I just had to.

I turned around quickly and screamed. I didn't see anything, just my reflection in the window but sometimes you just have to scream. Besides, it wasn't much of a scream. I'm capable of much more.

I figured it must have been my reflection in the window that I thought was staring at me. However, I wasn't going to take any chances. I decided to leave my room.

If it's one thing I can't stand, it's someone looking at me especially when I don't know who it is.

2

At this point I should say something nice about Booger, instead of just trashing him. Give me time — I'm thinking. He's very . . . he's very good with bugs . . . because he sort of looks like one. I'm kidding. Maybe Booger wouldn't be so bad if he wasn't my brother.

Anyway, Halloween was less than a week away. I hadn't totally firmed up my plans for the big night. I was working on it. I was planning on going trick-or-treating with one of my best friends, Hillary.

I'm now in sixth grade. It's probably one of my last years to go trick-or-treating. My dad thinks I'm getting too old to go this year.

After trick-or-treating we were going to go to the school Halloween carnival. The carnival is sometimes fun and sometimes boring. It depends on how many kids show up and what parents are helping put it on. If they have dumb games and don't do anything but shove food down your throat, it's pretty boring.

Last year we had a Monster Mash in one of the rooms. It was just a room to dance in, but because we were dressed up and it was Halloween they called it a Monster Mash. They were playing the song "The Monster Mash" every three minutes but then the tape player ate it.

The whole thing was weird because none of the dumb boys would come into the room. There were only about three boys who would darken the doorway and then all they wanted to do was slam dance. I actually thought that was okay, but some people got a little bent over it.

They try to do scary stuff at the carnival, but it isn't really scary. One time they told fortunes. Someone's mom dressed up like a gypsy and looked into a bowling ball and told you that you were going to get straight A's and brush your teeth after every meal and stupid things like that.

One of the cooler things they've had at the carnival is the booth where you stick your hand through a hole in a box to feel something and they say it's like brains but it's really spaghetti.

Jeff once pulled out a piece of spaghetti and ate it saying, "I love brains. Yum, they're my favorite."

Louise almost hurled the fourteen hot dogs she'd eaten. She said she knew it was spaghetti, she was just feeling ill. If you asked me, I bet she thought they were real brains and if she hadn't totally been pigging out and left some potato chips for someone else, she would've felt a whole lot better.

Last year David put the fourth-grade-class gerbil in the eyeball box. Of course the gerbil ate the grapes that were supposed to be eyeballs. Then Megan stuck her hand in the box, felt the moving, furry gerbil and knocked down the whole table trying to get her arm out. The gerbil got loose and it took us twenty minutes to catch it. That was a fun Halloween carnival.

One year they tried to show a scary movie but too many parents, including mine, complained. My mother has this thing about TV, videos, and video games. She says we should be having fun instead of being glued to a screen. She's probably right, but I do like scary movies, sometimes. It also seems like the perfect night to watch one, too.

And then there's the costume competition. I've never won. And it isn't really fair. You ought to see what some of the mothers do so their kids can win the best costume prize. My mother is lousy with costumes. She never wants to do what I want to do. She tries to help, but what she wants to do is always something too weird or stupid. One year she wanted me to be a box.

"A box?" I said. "Like just a box?"

"Yes," she said, "it'd be very original." And my dad is completely no help.

Every year he says, "Be a ghost."

A ghost has never won the best-costume award.

I do my own costumes. Besides being a princess or a fairy-tale lady like Sleeping Beauty or Rapunzel — I'd get a big wig — I thought of being Queen Elizabeth the First since we have the same name. I wasn't going to be the current Queen of England, but the one from a long, long time ago, that she was named after.

I asked my dad if that was who I was named after and he said, "No, we named you after your crazy great-aunt Elizabeth who made hats and Christmas decorations out of old toilet paper rolls."

"Thanks, Dad," I said.

I still tell everyone I'm named after a queen. It sounds better. I do like to make things, though. It probably goes with the name.

Anyway, I didn't know for sure what I wanted to be for Halloween. I could be Cinderella without even doing anything. I've already got the ugly clothes and I have to work all the time, too. Perfect.

Speaking of working all the time, I was supposed to be working on my report for school the next day but I had to go fold my clean clothes on my parents' bed. Then I had to go down and get the mail. Then I had to run over to the neighbors' and borrow some vanilla. Then I had to practice the cello, which I absolutely hate and want to quit but, of course, my parents won't let me.

My mother says, "You can play or not play when you grow up. Right now, you play. This is a wonderful opportunity that you'll thank me for some day."

I told her when I grow up I'm playing the electric guitar.

I set the table and turned off the light in the bathroom — like I was told. Then I was told to go get a can of pears in the basement. I hate the basement.

I know it shouldn't scare me. I know there is nothing down there. I've been told a thousand million times.

It still scares me. I hate going down in the basement by myself. I even hate going down there with someone else.

I told my mom, "Let's not have pears."

"Lizzie," she sighed, "just go get them. I'm right here. Leave the door open and it will only take you a second."

"Make Booker," I said, "he doesn't do anything around here."

"I'm asking *you*, Lizzie," said my mother.

I just looked at her wondering how much I could fight this.

She said, "You're going to ask me to do something for you and I'm going to remember when I asked you to get a little can of pears and you wouldn't do it."

I was trapped. I was losing no matter what I did. If I went downstairs I was going to be scared senseless and if I refused I was going to be in trouble forever. I hate it when you have no choice. Why do my parents think it's good for me to go downstairs to the basement?

My dad always says, "Face your fear and the death of fear is certain."

Wrong! Death *by* fear is more like it.

"Fine," I said. "I'm going but if I don't make it back, don't let Booker touch any of my stuff."

"Cut the dramatics, Elizabeth. Make sure you turn the lights off when you come back up."

That's the scariest part. There is one light at the top of the stairs that doesn't lighten anything. Then you have to go down the stairs and reach around the corner to turn on the other light switch that turns on the main basement lights.

Reaching around the corner to turn on the light takes every ounce of courage I have. All it would take would be for someone to touch my hand before I reached the switch and I would pass out on the spot. I mean it.

I turned on the light at the top of the stairway and started whistling. My mother told me that whistling made you not afraid. Take it from me, it doesn't work. I walked slowly and as quietly as

11

I could downstairs. If there was something there I didn't want them to know I was coming. I wanted to surprise them.

I reached the bottom and forced myself to ram my hand around the corner and turn on the light. I ran over and got the pears without even taking one breath. I made sure I flipped the light off before I bolted up the stairs to win a new world's record.

One time I missed the switch at the bottom. My body was running back upstairs before I could even think of doing it. I had to go back downstairs and turn it off. That was the worst.

This time I was running up the stairs and I was loud because it's okay to be loud when you're leaving. I didn't say anything, though.

My friend Allison, when she's alone in her house and then is going to leave, always yells. She says, "You better be gone by the time I get back."

I didn't say anything, but I heard something. It was an old woman's voice and it felt like it was whispering in my ear.

She said, "I'm going to get you."

I turned off the light and slammed the door.

I told my mother, "I'm never going down there again."

3

The next day I had a report due. My teacher, Mrs. Rose, had assigned us oral reports to do with a partner. Why do teachers do these things? I don't get the point. Why can't we do things by ourselves?

I got stuck with Brian. He is completely weird. The only thing he can talk about is electricity.

I mean it. You can ask him what time it is and he will tell you about the electricity stored in the battery of his watch. The guy is like in love with electricity.

We had our choice, we were supposed to do this great report on something about Halloween or we could tell a sort of scary folktale or fairy tale. It had to be old. I wanted to tell a story like any normal person would want to do. However, Brian, who isn't normal, was dying to give a report.

I said, "You've got to be kidding."

"No," he said.

"What do you want to give a report on?" I asked.

He said, "I'm not sure yet."

"Well," I said, "we're supposed to do this together."

"Okay," he said.

I said, "I think we better just tell a story."

He said, "No, no, let's give a report. Please?"

I knew what he was up to.

I said, "You better not talk about electricity or you're hamburger."

"Absolutely," he said, "you pick something and I'll do something cool along with it."

I looked at the list of suggested topics on our handout sheet. One of the topics listed was "The Origins of Jack-o'-Lanterns." I wasn't thrilled by the topic but it looked as good as the rest and I figured I could find something on it in the library. I told Brian.

He said, "That sounds good."

We had exactly one week to prepare our reports. I found some material right off in the library for my half. However, I didn't have a clue as to what Brian was going to do for his part.

"I have to know," I said, "what if we end up saying the same thing?"

"We won't," he said.

"I'm going to flunk and it's your fault," I said.

Then our reports were due. At least we both

showed up. That's a plus. I still didn't know what Brian was going to say.

Wouldn't you know it, Whitney and Lisa went first. They are perfect. Of course they picked telling a fairy tale.

They did it by using regular old store-bought Halloween masks to be the different people in the story. They acted it out and they'd practiced, too. It was totally cool. Everyone liked it. They were just perfect.

Mrs. Rose kept saying, "How clever."

They told the Grimms' fairy tale about the boy who was so stupid he didn't know how to be afraid. Nothing scared him. He wanted to learn how to make his skin crawl or get the shivers. He should have just gone to our basement.

People tried to scare him by dressing up as ghosts and showing him dead bodies and stuff, but he wasn't afraid. They got him to stay in a haunted castle that was full of all kinds of scary stuff but he didn't get scared. In fact, he beat everyone up, got the treasure buried in the castle, and married the princess.

He still wanted his skin to crawl. The princess finally granted his wish. She poured a bowl of goldfish on him while he slept. He woke up and said, "My skin is crawling."

It was a dumb ending. She could've just let him watch Booger pick his nose. *That* will make your skin crawl.

Anyway, the teacher loved it. They were perfect. They always do really cool stuff and it's never messy.

Mrs. Rose asked us what we thought the point of the story was. I wanted to say that the point of this for me was to make sure I got either Whitney or Lisa for a partner next time, but I didn't. Renee thought it meant that goldfish were scary. Wake up, Renee.

We pretty much agreed that it meant that even if you're stupid it's better not to be afraid. When you are afraid, it doesn't seem like you can think as well. All you can think about is being afraid. Anyway, the guy wasn't completely stupid. He got the treasure and the princess. I felt sorry for the princess, though. It didn't seem like she got much of a prize.

It was our turn.

Brian said, "Ladies first."

I was in flunk city. I could feel it for sure.

"Gee, thanks," I said.

I started telling about how jack-o'-lanterns got their name. I wished I'd thought of something cool like using masks or something, except whatever I made would've looked dorky. Anyway, I just stood there and read my report on the Irish legend of how jack-o'-lanterns got their name. I'm going to tell you because it's sort of interesting.

There was this guy named Jack. He was walking down the road and he saw the devil. He knew the devil was there to get his soul because Jack was selfish and mean. By the side of the road was an apple tree with these great big juicy apples.

Jack tricked the devil into climbing the tree to pick the biggest juiciest apples on top and, while he was up there, Jack carved a cross on the trunk of the tree. With the cross there, the devil couldn't climb down.

The devil told Jack if he would let him down, he wouldn't come for him for another ten years. Jack wouldn't do it. He told the devil he would only let him down if he promised to never come back to get his soul. The devil agreed.

Pretty soon Jack got really old and died and his soul went up to heaven, but they wouldn't let him in because he was so dang mean and selfish. That's when he went down to see the devil but he couldn't get in there either because of the promise the devil had made.

Jack asked where he should go and the devil told him to go back to earth. Jack said he couldn't find his way in the dark. The devil threw him a hot coal from the fire and Jack caught it and put it inside a turnip he was chewing on. From then on he's been walking around with his jack-o'-lantern looking for a resting place. He's still mean and selfish.

So the first jack-o'-lanterns were carved out of

turnips, but when people got to America they thought pumpkins were easier and better to carve than turnips. They switched to pumpkins.

That was the end of my part of the report.

Mrs. Rose asked, "Did you bring a carved turnip, Lizzie?"

"No," I said.

I can't do anything right. If I'd been Lisa or Whitney I would've made individual turnips for everyone in the class. I would've made talking turnips with dresses and wigs. I would've brought a barbecue with hot coals and roasted turnips for everyone.

Mrs. Rose just smiled at me.

"Brian?" she said.

He started, "One of things you think about when you see jack-o'-lanterns and Halloween stuff is thunder and lightning. They're supposed to be scary, but they are really electricity."

I could've screamed. He went and talked for an hour about, you guessed it, electricity.

Mrs. Rose said thank you. I was sure she was going to say you both will have to repeat this grade.

"Brian," she said, "that was an unusual connection you made between Halloween and electricity. Wasn't it, class?"

They didn't answer. They were asleep.

4

I was in a great mood because of Brian, Mr. Electricity, and then Scott started picking on me. Scott's got a problem. He's always picking on people.

He's always saying stuff to me like, "Way to go, stupid," when I get asked a question and I don't know where we are.

He's also always calling me names and stuff. He picks on other kids, too. It really ticks me off. He's really sneaky about it and doesn't usually get caught.

Well, we were doing art. Right then, we were working on our terra-cotta figurines. Scott was like jabbing his elbow into Blake every time the teacher wasn't looking and it was making me mad. Blake is the littlest kid in our class because he got to skip a grade and Scott is always shoving him around. Blake wasn't saying anything because he was trying to be macho about it.

I finally said, "Why don't you lay off?"

He said, "Why don't you mind your own business?"

I said, "Blake is my friend and that makes it my business."

He kind of laughed and grunted at me. Then he moved closer and started looking at my sculpture.

"Do you mind?" I said.

"What is that?" he said. "It looks dumb."

I said, "It is none of your business, but if you have to know it's a rabbit."

He started laughing through his nose. I gave him the dirtiest look I could.

He said to John, "Look at this pile of manure that Lizzie is making," and he poked at my rabbit with his finger totally ruining it.

Honestly, at this point I wasn't that mad. I wasn't even really thinking. All I did was pick up a very small pile of wet clay and shove it in his mouth. Of course, he being the total jerk he is, had to pick up a huge pile and throw it at me. That was all. Was anyone hurt? No.

However, the teacher decided to look up right then and we both got sent to the principal's office. There we sat outside forever waiting to get in. We waited outside her office where everyone walks by and knows you're in trouble and are waiting to get in.

While we were there, sitting on the bench, this totally weird thing happened. This totally ugly woman came by. I mean ugly. She had a nose you could hang clothes on. She stopped and looked at us.

She laughed at us.

Then she looked straight at me and said, "You can't do anything right. You're no good."

It was weird that she said that. It was also weird that her voice, something in the way she talked, made me feel funny. She left, walking out the front door.

"Who was that?" said Scott.

"How should I know?" I said.

"Then why did she say that to you?" he said.

"Well, maybe she was saying it to you," I said.

"Hardly," he said.

Then we were called into the principal's office. We were told that our violent actions during art were considered a major offense and she was going to have to call our parents. Plus, we had to report to noon detention for a week.

You want to know what the dumbest part was? She didn't even ask us what happened. She just chewed us out.

We both told her "thank you," but I have no idea what for. What? Like we were having such a terrific time? Things get pretty insane inside the principal's office.

So then I had to figure out how I was going to break the news to my parents before the principal called. I knew I was really going to get it, but if I told them first, I figured it might be slightly better.

I was mad at myself. I thought, Why do these things always happen to me? What is wrong with me?

Then I remembered that weird lady. I could hear her say, "You're no good."

I wondered why anyone would say that. She didn't know me. I was depressed but I made it through the rest of school. Everyone was talking about me. No one would play with me at afternoon recess except Marie.

She said, "Let's go beat up some boys!"

Don't worry. We played on the tire swing instead. I may be crazy, but I'm not a maniac.

What bothered me most was some of my so-called friends were totally ignoring me. They acted as if I were so awful that they might catch something from me. They looked at me as if they'd never gotten in trouble before.

Blake came up and thanked me. He was pretty upset. I think it must be hard to be the littlest.

My mom picked Booger and me up at school.

"How was school, you two?"

I didn't have to say anything because Booger went on for a half hour telling her about Halloween fire safety, like anyone would care. Then when we thought he was done he repeated the whole thing.

"We're not stupid," I said to him, "we heard you the first time and I promise I won't light my costume on fire."

"Lizzie, be nice," my mom said. "Booker is excited about learning new things, aren't you, Booker."

"Yes," he said and he stuck his tongue out at me and of course my mother didn't see it.

Usually I would have told on him. However, I thought that under the circumstances, it could wait. I knew I needed to tell her right away that she was going to get a call from "you know who," but I didn't want to do it in front of Booger. It was none of his business.

My mom said, "I have to make a couple of stops on the way home. I hope it's okay."

I said, "Great."

I was going to ask if the answering machine was on, but I thought it would be too suspicious. Besides, the principal always calls back. You can never get out of these things. When you get in trouble you're completely trapped. You spend all your time trying to find a way out but there isn't a way out. You just have to live through it.

5

We went to the grocery store. Booker and I begged to buy pumpkins while we were there. I tried to tell my mom that jack-o'-lanterns were originally turnips, but I don't think she heard me.

She kept saying "oh really?" like she was interested but I think what she wanted to do was get out of the grocery store as fast as possible.

Booger is the one that finally got her. He said, "Please Mom, *please.* We have to get pumpkins today or we won't get them. There's hardly any time left anyway."

"All right," she said, "stop begging. Please don't get any that are too big or too heavy."

"Okay, Mom," we said and went to pick them out.

We picked out the two biggest pumpkins in the whole place. We had to have one shopping cart just to hold our pumpkins.

When Mom saw us she said, "That's exactly what I didn't want you to do. Go get a smaller one and meet me at the checkout stand."

"Cool," said Booger, "now we'll have three."

I started to say, "I don't think that's what she meant," but then thought, what's the worst thing that can happen?

We picked out an adorable little pumpkin. It was bigger than a turnip but still perfect for a nice little jack-o'-lantern. Of course my mother had a fit when we got to the checkout stand. She didn't dare lose her place in line though and it was almost her turn so we didn't have time to get them back. We got to keep them all.

"You two," she said. "Never again."

"Mom," I said, "it's Halloween, show some spirit."

"To me," she said, "it is All Hallows' Eve, the evening before All Saints' Day, when we honor those who have died."

"Whatever," I said.

"Goodness, Lizzie, these aren't pumpkins, they're mobile homes. You could live in one."

"We could put Booker in one and let him live in it out back," I said.

"Very funny," he said.

"Don't start anything," my mother said.

I didn't. I just finished it off a little.

I sang, "Lizzie, Lizzie, pumpkin eater, had a

brother and wouldn't keep him. Put him in a pumpkin shell and there she kept him very well."

Booger was ignoring me and I thought I was pretty hysterical. The least he could do was say something back. He kept ignoring me. I considered singing louder but remembering what had happened earlier that day I sang it again but quietly.

My mother said, "Elizabeth, stop it."

We next went to the mall. That's guaranteed to make my mother cranky.

"This will only take a minute," my mom said, "I have two errands to run. Stick close. No one get sidetracked."

Right off Booger talked her into looking at the raisin costumes.

Luckily she said, "Oh, let's not this year, how about a cowboy?"

"I did it last year," said Booger.

"Then maybe you should be a pirate this year," suggested my mom.

"Okay," said Booger.

I can't believe it. Why does he give up so easy? Either something is wrong with him or I'm totally weird.

I would never have given up even if I didn't want to be a stupid raisin anymore. I would've fought, cried, and pouted until I got my way. Little kids just don't have what it takes anymore.

We went past this strange-looking store.

"Look Mom," I said, "it's a new store."

"You're right," she said, "what is it?"

The windows were covered so you couldn't see in and there was only a small paper sign above the entrance. It said RALPH'S HALLOWEEN STORE.

My mom didn't want to go in.

I said, "Mom, it's a new store. We're obligated to check it out."

We went in. Inside there were all kinds of Halloween masks and decorations. There was scary organ music playing in the background.

A man came up to us.

"If it isn't Lizzie," he said, "and well, it's Booker, isn't it."

He winked at me.

Booker said, "How do you know us?"

"Booker," my mom said.

"I'm sorry," he said to my mom. "I'm Ralph. I sold you a Christmas tree. You must have forgotten. That happens. I usually don't make a lasting impression."

However, I did sort of remember him. My brain actually hurt as I felt it trying to match this guy up with a memory. I could remember but I couldn't remember what I remembered. I know it doesn't make sense.

"I remember you," I said.

"Don't worry about it," he said. "That's what happens. You remember then you forget and then you remember. You'll remember probably when you don't want to."

We all laughed but it wasn't funny.

"Now, what can I get you or are you just looking today?"

"Looking," said my mom. She glanced at her watch. "Oh my, we don't have time to do anything today. Come on, kids."

We headed toward the door. I was last in line.

Ralph said, "Lizzie, just a minute."

I turned around.

He said, "I can't go with you this time, but remember you aren't alone. Remember you don't have to be perfect. You just have to be Lizzie. Things aren't always what they seem."

"Okay," I said. I wondered why he wanted to go with us.

"Trick or treat," he said.

"Happy Halloween," I said.

We ran to the pharmacy and then back out to the parking lot. My mom almost ran two lights trying to get home fast. I almost forgot what was waiting for me when I got home.

We walked in the door and my dad said, "Elizabeth, you have some explaining to do."

My mother looked at me with this hopeless look.

"Now what?" she said.

Her mouth was sort of hanging open and eyes were drooping. I don't know how she does those faces. She should go on one of those shows on TV for people that can do weird things. She'd be the mom with the funniest faces.

"Okay," I said, "before you panic, you should know that it all started with electricity."

6

I was French toast. My parents grounded me, of course, but they couldn't decide for how long or exactly from what. I guess I was just grounded in general.

My dad was a little better than my mom. He was at least sort of irritated at the principal because she told him that young women do not solve their differences by using violence. He told her that he wasn't defending my actions but he wasn't sure that shoving clay in Scott's mouth was exactly a violent act. He saw it as more of a defensive act.

"Exactly," I said.

He said, "Lizzie, you better stay out of this."

My mom said, "Phil, you're being ridiculous. You know exactly what happened. Lizzie has a temper. She doesn't think before she acts and she doesn't know when to quit."

"Mom," I said, trying not to cry, "that isn't true. It was his fault."

"Please don't blame anyone else. I don't care what he was doing. I care about what you were doing. Your judgment was faulty. You could've done something else," my mom said.

"I was just trying to help Blake," I said.

"Getting in trouble didn't help anyone," my mother said.

I'd had it. I started crying.

"Great," I said, "I'm so awful, why don't you just get rid of me."

"Knock it off, Lizzie," my dad said.

That's when I went to my room. It had been a long day. I just couldn't take anymore.

As I walked down the hall, my mother said, "Lizzie, we'll talk about this after dinner."

We didn't. They got busy and I did my homework. I went to bed and fell asleep trying to remember what Ralph had said to me in the store.

I told myself that if I remembered I should write it down. I had a dream. Actually, I had a nightmare.

I dreamt I was standing at the top of the stairs going to the basement. I was reaching to turn the light on but it was too far away. I reached even further and lost my balance. I started falling. I fell and fell like I was falling down a deep dark well. I never hit bottom because I woke up.

My parents seemed okay in the morning. They didn't say anything except my dad said, "Don't

31

hurt anyone," when he went out the door to work. He was smiling so I think it was a joke.

Every year the local radio station puts on a Haunted House. You know, where you pay money and you walk through an old house and they try to scare you to death. It's supposed to be guaranteed to give you bad dreams for a month. Booger was begging my mom to take him that night.

She looked at me, not Booger, as if I put him up to it, and said, "We'll have to see."

I figured that if they went, I'd get left at home. I went to school. On the bus a bunch of kids were talking about the Haunted House. It made me feel sad because I really wanted to go. I was so mad at Scott.

They were also talking about what they were going to dress up as. Lisa asked me what I was going to be and I said I was thinking about being Queen Elizabeth the First.

"That's cool," said Lisa, "to be someone with your name."

"I thought it would be sort of fun," I said.

"You shouldn't be a queen," said Scott, who was listening when it was none of his business. "You should be another Lizzie all right, but you should be Lizzie Borden."

A bunch of kids laughed. I didn't get it. I didn't know who Lizzie Borden was.

"She killed her parents," said Lisa, "with an ax.

She's really famous. She's in the encyclopedia. I did a report on her once."

She was right, of course. When I got to school I went to the library and looked her up in the encyclopedia. She was under Borden, Lizzie Andrew. At least my middle name isn't a boy's name.

It said she was accused of killing her stepmother and her father with an ax. The courts found her not guilty but everyone else thought she did it for sure. At the time of her trial, some jerk like Scott made up a little rhyme that stuck forever.

Lizzie Borden took an ax
And gave her mother forty whacks;
When she saw what she had done,
She gave her father forty-one.

I guess it's one way to get famous. I tried to find someone creepy with the name Scott in the encyclopedia but I ran out of time. The bell rang and I had to go to class.

I was more determined than ever to be Queen Elizabeth for Halloween. I decided I'd work on my costume right after school. I worked really hard to get my work done in class so I wouldn't have any homework.

Mrs. Rose even smiled at me at the end of the day. I'm not saying it meant anything. It was just nice.

I was the first one home. Booger rides a different bus and it's always late.

I walked in the house and said, "I'm home."

There was no answer. There was a note on the refrigerator.

Lizzie and Booker,

I'll be home at 5:30 pm. No friends over. No TV.

Lizzie, get your homework done. Wash your hands before you eat anything. Please leave the answering machine on and don't erase my messages. Do not, I repeat, do not fight.

Love you,
Mom

Booger walked in the door.

He screamed, "Mom!"

"You stupid idiot," I said, "she's not home. There's a note on the fridge. You're supposed to wash your hands."

"You're not the boss of me," he said.

"I would never want to be your boss," I said. "I'm going to work on my costume so just stay out of my way and don't bug me or I'm telling."

He looked at me like he wanted to slug me.

"Don't even think about it," I said.

He went to his room and did whatever it is he does in there. I don't want to know. I went upstairs, climbed the steps to the attic, and pushed open the door. I'm usually not afraid of the attic. It's like the opposite of the basement.

It smelled like dust. You could see the dust particles in the sunlight coming through the window. I pulled the cord on the bare light bulb. It worked. That was a miracle. It's usually burned out.

I went to the costume box. My mom saves anything strange that we might use for a costume. I started digging.

I found a perfect red dress. I think it was my mom's prom dress or something. I looked like a queen. It hung clear down to the floor.

I really needed a crown. There were no crowns in the box but I did find a big piece of red velvet-looking stuff. I kind of thought I could maybe make a cape from it. I changed my mind. It looked too ratty. Queens should not look ratty.

I figured I could make a crown from some construction paper. I knew we had some glitter somewhere I could use on it. I thought I could even write Queen Elizabeth on it just so the stupid people would be sure to know who I was.

There's an old stand-up mirror there and I put the dress on and looked at myself. I wasn't totally impressed. I guessed I'd look better with the crown and some makeup I'd borrow from my mom.

While I was looking in the mirror I picked up

a witch's hat I'd tossed out of the box. I was trying to remember when I'd last been a witch. Just for fun, I was going to put the hat on with the queen dress.

I put my hand into the witch's hat to straighten out the point. The door to the attic creaked and then shut all by itself. I was startled but I wasn't really scared. I thought it could be a draft or something.

"Booger, is that you? You're not funny at all," I said.

Then I smoothed out the brim of the hat. I heard something move in the corner of the room by my old rocking horse. That made me extremely nervous. I thought it was a mouse. I hate mice.

Then when I put the hat on my head, a cloud moved in front of the sun and the light bulb decided to burn out. I freaked. I did a major scream. I made my way to the door and ran out of there slamming it behind me and almost tripped down the steps to the attic with the stupid dress on.

My mother came running upstairs. She'd just gotten home.

"Lizzie, what is wrong?" she asked. "It sounded like the house was caving in."

"Mom," I said, trying to catch my breath, "I was just scared to death. I was upstairs and I put on the witch's hat and the room went totally black and I thought I was going to lose it."

My mother went up the stairs and opened the door to the attic. The light was on.

"Lizzie," she yelled, "you left the light on and stuff strewn from one end of this room to the other. Do something right. Get up here and clean it up. Turn off the light when you're done."

"But Mom," I said.

She said, "I don't want to hear it."

"Can I take off this dress first?"

"Please do," she said.

7

Get this. We went to the Haunted House and I got to go. I didn't ask any questions. I didn't want to risk it. You never know what a parent is going to do.

We drove over to the place where they had it this year. It was almost across town. They change the location every year. The places they hold it usually get torn down from one year to the next.

This year it was in an old, totally huge house. It looked pretty scary from the outside. They were blaring scary music with screams in it. It was one of those haunted house tapes you can buy.

I could tell Booger was scared.

He said, "I hope they don't have a gorilla. I hate gorillas."

I was only hoping that one of my friends was there. It was pretty dorky going to a haunted house with your mother. Normally, I would've asked to bring a friend. However, since I was already in trouble, it would have been stupid to push it.

Dad paid and we all headed for the front door.

"We're all going?" I asked.

"Yeah," said my dad, "it's a family thing."

"Okay," I said. I'd planned on going in with Booger and ditching him.

They had laid out the house so you went through two rooms downstairs, went upstairs through three rooms, then down a back stairway into the kitchen and out the back door. In the first room they had someone in a gorilla suit in a cage grabbing at you. It reached for Booger but he was flat against the wall trying to slide out of the room.

It got my mom, which was cool. She wouldn't scream though. She just did this stupid kind of laugh like she didn't know what to do, which she didn't.

I finally said, "You're suppposed to scream, Mom."

She let rip this squeaky little wimp scream and the gorilla let go and went after someone else.

"Isn't this funny?" she said.

Next they had this sort of dumb room. It was called the Shadow Room. I mean, it had a sign that said it was the Shadow Room. It had a bunch of slow flashing lights on one wall which made you have really big clear shadows on the opposite wall.

It wasn't very scary. People were mostly doing

kind of goofy things, lifting their legs and stuff, making bunnies with their fingers. My dad was getting into it. He used his fingers to make it look like he had antlers.

"You make a cool moose, Dad," I said.

Then I looked at my shadow. I wasn't doing anything. I mean it. I wasn't moving any part of my body, but my shadow was waving at me. I looked behind me to make sure no one was there. I even counted the people in the room and the shadows to make sure it was mine.

I said to my dad, "Dad, why is my shadow waving at me?"

He looked and it stopped.

"What?" he said.

"Nothing," I said.

"Let's move on," said my mom.

"I'm ready," I said.

I looked at my shadow one more time. It gave me the thumbs-up sign. I ran out of the room, shoving myself into Booger. Of course he made a huge deal about it.

My mother snapped. "Elizabeth," she said through clenched teeth.

"Sorry," I said, "I didn't mean to."

"You never mean to," said my mother.

"Sorry," I said again.

We headed upstairs. It was pretty boring. There was a Mummy Room, a Dracula Room, and a Mad Scientist Room. All were extremely fakey but I could tell Booger was afraid.

We went downstairs into the kitchen where a witch was cooking. It was pretty funny. They had a bunch of people with their heads sticking through platters on tables so it looked like they were dinner. One guy had an apple in his mouth.

"I bet that gets tiring," my mom said.

We were going out the back door. There was sort of a back porch thing. Someone was poking me in the back. I thought it was Booger.

I said, "Knock it off."

He kept doing it so I turned around to let him have it. It wasn't Booger. It was the ugly woman from school who had talked to me while I was waiting to go into the principal's office. I'm here to tell you, she is ugly and she is scary looking.

She had the worst breath you can imagine and I could tell because she was extremely close to me.

She said, "Shall I tell you what you really are?"

I said, "No, thank you," and tried to move away.

"Why don't you go down to the basement?" she said.

I turned around and yelled, "Dad!"

He said, "I'm right here. What's wrong?"

"This woman," I said and pointed to where she was.

She was gone.

"She was just here."

My dad was laughing.

"Guess you got spooked, Lizzie," he said.

"No," I said, "you don't understand."

I heard a woman's laugh and I didn't like the way it sounded.

8

On the way home they dropped the bomb. My mom was the one that pushed the button.

"Lizzie," she said, "we've decided that your punishment for your actions at school will be the following."

I thought, the following, like more than one?

"We realize," she continued, "that you have detention at school but we also want you to be sure you think about it before you pull a stunt like that again."

"So," said my dad, "to be very nice, we're letting you go trick-or-treating but you can't go with friends. If you want to go, you have to go with Booker. He needs someone to go with him and you can help out by being with him."

"Why doesn't he go with his own friends?" I said.

"That's a possibility," said my mom, "but he still needs someone older along."

I thought, I'm not going trick-or-treating with Booger's friends.

"I don't think it's much of a punishment," said my dad.

I did.

I said, "What if Booker doesn't want me to go with him?"

"We asked him," said my mom, "and it's all right with him, isn't it, Booker?"

The little creep said, "yes," and smiled at me.

"What if I just don't go trick-or-treating?" I asked.

"That's fine," said my dad, "but I don't think going to the carnival is even a possibility if you're going to have that kind of attitude."

"This is unfair," I said, "and it's stupid. Why should I have to go with him?"

"Because," said my mother, "I have to go over and help set up for the carnival and your dad needs to stay home and answer the door."

"I'll answer the door," I said. I couldn't imagine trick-or-treating with my little brother. Talk about boring.

"Lizzie," said my dad, "I'm getting angry. You're grounded and we're trying to give you a break here and you act like it's a worse punishment."

"Sorry," I said. I wanted to scream it but I didn't.

The subject got dropped. It was going to be the worst Halloween ever. I wasn't going to have fun. I was going trick-or-treating with the Booger.

The last thing my mom said was, "I thought you'd be grateful you got to go. We could have just said you were staying home. How do you think this makes Booker feel? Is this the way a big sister acts?"

How do you answer that? I wanted to tell them it wasn't my fault. I wanted to tell them that punishing me at all was stupid. You know what? I knew it wouldn't do any good. I told myself I didn't want to go anyway. I was getting too old.

Then for some ridiculous reason I started thinking about my friend Mary. Last year we went trick-or-treating and she was wearing this really long black shirt thing she'd sewn herself. She was a witch.

I accidentally stepped on her dress as we were going up some stairs on these people's sidewalk and she fell down and it ripped her dress completely apart and she was on the ground with just her underpants on. When she got up she had to hold her skirt around her like a towel.

At the next house we said, "Trick or treat and do you have any safety pins?"

It was pretty funny if you'd been there. Anyway, I was laughing about it to myself.

My mother said, "Elizabeth, it isn't funny."

"What?" I said.

She gave me that look. The kind of look that says don't even think of saying anything.

"Fine," I said. "I won't even talk. I won't do anything. I won't breathe."

"Will too," said Booger. "You have to."

I thought about taking him trick-or-treating and losing him.

The next day at school I got asked by at least four kids that live around us to go out trick-or-treating with them. I told them I probably wasn't going.

"Why?" they asked.

"I just don't feel like it this year," I said.

It made me sad to say it. I wanted to go. Halloween was wrecked.

I couldn't seem to do anything right all day. I messed up my math paper and got asked to redo it. I left my health book at home. All my pencils were dull. I came in practically last in PE during our regular run and I'm usually one of the first.

When I got home my mom was all cheerful.

"How about we get those pumpkins carved?" she said.

Booger acted like he had won the lottery.

My mother laid newspapers everywhere. I had something sticky on my shoe and the paper was sticking to it.

"Elizabeth," my mother said.

I tried to cut teeth in my pumpkin's mouth and

46

completely loused it up. I kept having to make the mouth bigger and bigger to fix it. It looked so awful I just wanted to throw it away.

My mother kept saying, "It looks fine. It looks scarier that way."

"It looks horrible," I said. "I can't do anything right."

"That's not true, Lizzie, let's not feel sorry for ourself," said my mom.

I ate a whole bag of chips.

Booger's pumpkin turned out perfectly because, of course, my mother helped him.

It isn't fair.

My pumpkin had this giant clown mouth and these little tiny eyes because I didn't have any room to make them and this square nose because I couldn't cut it right. It looked major bad. I put a candle in it and tried to put the lid back on. I had forgotten to cut the lid at an angle so the lid fell right through.

I started crying. I wanted to pick up that pumpkin and throw it against the wall. My mom put her arm around me.

"What's wrong, Lizzie?" she said.

"I can't do anything right," I said. "I've ruined my whole life."

"Oh, Lizzie," she said, "you just made some mistakes. Life is full of them. You learn from them. I love you, mistakes and all."

I just kept crying.

9

It was Halloween Day. It was a school day this year. We were doing math. At least we were supposed to be doing math.

Right then and there in math class I remembered something. I wrote it down.

"You don't have to be perfect. You have to be Lizzie. Things aren't always what they seem."

I'd finally remembered what Ralph had said to me. I was wishing I could remember something else about him. It had something to do with our Christmas tree and my mother.

Right then I got asked a question. Why do teachers ask you questions when they know you're not paying attention? I had no idea what we were doing.

"Trick or treat, Elizabeth," she said. "Let's try to keep our mind on math. Could we?"

"I'll try," I said.

After lunch we got to help set up the lunch room

for the carnival. I got to help make floating ghosts with helium ballons. Of course I was doing it with Michelle, the school's best artist, and hers looked perfect. Mine looked like rain clouds, which is what Brian, Mr. Electricity, called them.

"No, you moron, they're ghosts," I said.

"Oh," he said. "Do you know what causes lightning?"

"Yes," I said, "you told me."

We had an emergency. Annie is the girl who I really feel sorry for. She has to wear her head gear for her braces all day long. She looks like she's from outer space and kids make fun of her.

Anyway, she bumped heads with Linda and they were both crying. Annie had cut her lips from her braces and was bleeding all over the place. A guy named Howard had to put his head between his legs because the blood was making him feel like he was going to faint or puke or both.

They had to get the school nurse, who had to go back and get her gloves on because of the blood, and in the meantime we just stood there and watched Annie. Finally they took her out of the room.

The nurse came back in and said she wouldn't have to have stitches. We were relieved. Poor Linda had a headache. Everyone was so wigged out about Annie that they forgot about her.

The room was pretty much decorated by then,

which was a good thing. If I say so myself, it looked pretty cool. Someone asked if we could turn off the lights and leave on just the spotlights to see what it looked like. They let us.

It looked even better. I was standing sort of apart from some of my friends. For some reason I looked over at the wall beside me. There was my shadow.

Get this though. There was no light shining where I was to make a shadow. However, there was my shadow.

Not only was my shadow where it wasn't supposed to be, my shadow was waving at me again. I had to blink my eyes about fifteen times before it would go away.

I know I probably should have pointed it out to someone, but what would I have said? "Hey, look at my dumb shadow waving at me."

Sorry. It wouldn't have worked. What if I was the only one who could see it? Then they would've thought I was crazy.

The only thing I could think of was that I probably had a brain tumor and I was seeing things. I figured everyone would feel badly about how they treated me when they found out I was dying. Then I figured that my mother would bury me in the ugly blue dress she bought me. Then they'd give Booger my room and my toys.

"No way," I said, forgetting where I was, "I'm not dying."

"That's a good plan," said Mrs. Rose who was walking by.

"Sorry," I said, "I was just thinking of a book I read."

I know it was a weak recovery but it was the best I could do.

10

I had to face it. The time had come. I couldn't lie to myself.

I wanted to go trick-or-treating badly. I wanted to go really bad. I'd do anything to go.

I decided I'd even go with Booger. I'd even try to be nice. Everyone was going trick-or-treating and I just had to.

I told my mom, "I'll take Booger."

"Elizabeth!"

"Sorry, I mean Booker. I just made a mistake," I said.

"No more mistakes," she said.

"Okay," I said.

"All right," she said, "let's have an early dinner so you two can go out and have a good time. It'll be fun. When you're grown up, think of how fondly you'll remember going out on Halloween with your little brother."

If she only knew.

I still had to make my crown. Of course we

didn't have any gold paper. We didn't even have yellow. We didn't have anything but white. We also didn't have any glitter. At least I couldn't find it and my mother didn't think we'd ever had any.

I made one. I made it out of white paper and drew some jewels on it. It looked stupid. The points on it were crooked and gnarly.

"Oh well," I said, "it's the thought that counts."

I could hear something in me say, "You can't do anything right."

I figured I'd cover up the flaws in my costume by wearing lots of makeup.

"Mom?" I yelled downstairs.

"Yes," she said reading my mind, "you can use my makeup, but don't leave a mess."

"Thanks Mom," I said.

I got all dressed up and came downstairs.

"Oh," said my mother.

"You look ravishing," said my dad.

"Maybe you have on too much makeup," said my mom.

"Who are you?" said Booger.

"I'm a raisin," I said.

"Huh?" he said.

"I'm Elizabeth the First, Queen of England," I said.

"You don't look like a queen," he said.

I was going to say you don't look like a pirate but he sort of did. It doesn't take much to be a pirate. All you need is a scarf on your head and an eye patch. Of course he got my mom to help him with his costume.

"You look very queenly," said my dad.

I felt better.

"Mom, can I borrow a pair of high heels?" I asked.

"Oh, honey, I don't think so. You'll be walking around. I'm afraid you'll hurt yourself."

"But Mom," I said. "I look stupid in my running shoes."

"My darling Elizabeth, you look sensible. It runs in the family. All the Queens of England wore sensible shoes. It must be genetic," my dad said.

"They didn't either," I said, "and no one will figure out I'm a queen."

"You're just fishing for compliments, Lizzie. You're fine," said my mom.

"I wasn't either," I said.

My dad leaned over to me.

"I'm glad you're going with Booker," he said.

We tried to eat dinner but it was ridiculous. Every year they say we can't go out before we eat, but we're way too excited to eat. We bolt down our dinner which is probably worse than not eating at all. While we were being force-fed, my dad lectured us on the evils of candy.

He even went into the story of Hansel and Gretel. He reminded us of what eating candy did to them and could do to everyone else.

"What?" said Booger.

"Well," said my dad, "it brings the witch out and she tries to make you fat and throw you into the oven."

I said, being nice, "Don't worry. The sister saves the brother from the witch."

Right then the door blew open.

"Booker," my mom said, "go close the door. Would everyone remember to close the door tightly?"

My dad said, "I didn't know the wind was even blowing tonight. Did you hear it?"

"No," I said.

11

Of course my mother had to take our picture. She had to take our picture five hundred times. Then she discovered her flash wasn't working so she had to take it some more.

Then she said, "Remember when you and Alicia were mummies?"

I try to forget. Alicia and I were going to be mummies and we thought we were brilliant because we did it with toilet paper. We wrapped each other up with plain rolls of toilet paper. It took forever.

We unrolled and wrapped it carefully around each other and then taped it. We actually didn't look half bad. That is, until we went outside.

It rained that year. It didn't just rain, it poured. It dumped tons of water.

We walked through the neighborhood in piles of soggy toilet paper. I can't even describe what we looked like. We didn't look like mummies. It felt just gross.

It seemed like every door we went up to, the people looked at us and said, "Oh my."

Then they gave us lots of candy. I figure they felt sorry for us. If you plan on trying it, check the weather report. Also think about carrying an umbrella.

Luckily my mom ran out of film so we got out the door. Booger and I were going trick-or-treating, the perfect little brother and big sister.

My mother said, "Only go for an hour. Stay just around here. When you get back, your dad will run you over to the carnival. I'll be there waiting for you."

"Okay," I said.

Booger and I fought immediately about which direction to go.

I finally said, "Listen you idiot. You're going to do what I say or I'm going to do something drastic."

"Like what?" he said.

"You don't want to know," I said.

He said, "I'll tell Mom."

"It won't do any good," I told him. "I'll tell on you, too."

We stood there. Neither of us would budge. It was a standoff.

He said, "Okay, we'll go your direction but then we'll go mine."

I had figured we'd head down our street to the west about three blocks and then work our way back. I didn't care what the little wart wanted to do. What did he know about trick-or-treating anyway?

"Remember to say thank you," I said when we went to the first house.

"Stop being a mother," he said, "or I'm telling."

"Just say thank you or I'm telling."

He did.

While walking to the next house he kept repeating, "Trick or treat. Smell my feet. Give me something good to eat."

He said it at least four hundred times. Well, it seemed like that many.

"Stop saying that," I said, "you're driving me crazy."

"I'll say what I want," said Booger and he said it again.

I told myself to just ignore him and concentrate on what I was doing, which was getting as much candy as I could in one hour's time. I felt like I was on one of those TV shows with a store and the clock running and you have a shopping cart and you have to get as much as you can in it before they call time.

"Hurry up," I said, "we've got work to do."

I was glad I didn't wear the high heels. I would've been much slower. We went to a house where the people were dressed up. They're usually good houses to go to. You know the places, they're all decorated and you can tell the people are really into it. Even if they don't give out lots of great candy, it's still more fun.

"Look honey," said a woman who was dressed up like a bee, "it's a gypsy and a pirate."

I said, "I'm not a gypsy. I'm the Queen of England."

"Oh," she said, "that's disappointing. I thought you were a fortune-telling gypsy. Do you want to tell my fortune?"

I said, "I'm the Queen of England. She doesn't tell fortunes."

"That's too bad," she said. "Well, Happy Halloween."

"A gypsy," I said under my breath.

"Maybe you have on too much makeup," said Booger.

"Maybe you should keep your mouth shut and walk faster," I said.

We got to the corner and Booger wanted to hang a right. I said "no," that we were going to go straight. He said he was going right with or without me. I seriously thought about letting him.

I was going to say, "Go ahead. See you at home," but I didn't. Wasn't I a good big sister?

I took a deep breath while he kept walking and then said, "Okay, but only for three houses."

We turned the corner. Now I know it was night, and things look different at night, but this looked really different. I thought I knew our neighborhood really well. I mean, I'd played here my whole life. However, the houses didn't look familiar, at all.

I got a little freaked out.

"Booger," I said, "let's turn around."

I noticed most of the houses didn't have lights on. It looked like most of the houses were very old and abandoned.

"Where did this fog come from?" I said.

There was like this low fog on the ground. Booger thought it was great. "You are so stupid," I said. "I'm turning around and I hope you get lost."

Then the streetlights went out.

"Booger," I said, "this is getting freaky. I'm turning around, seriously."

He was getting freaked out, too.

"Okay," he said.

I said, "Do you notice there are no other kids on the street?"

Know what? We held hands. Fear does strange things to you. We were power-walking.

There was a house right next to us that we hadn't noticed. It had tons of Halloween decorations and lots of lights on and believe it or not it had a big banner above the front porch that said, "Lots of candy. Get it here." It was a big house, at least three stories high.

"Let's go," said Booger.

"No," I said, "let's get out of here."

"Just one house," he said. "It isn't scary."

He was right. It was the only thing that didn't look scary. Right that second, the streetlights came back on.

"See," said Booger, "let's go in."

We walked up to the front porch.

"Ring the doorbell," I said.

There was a black cat on the porch. It didn't look friendly. Booger rang the doorbell.

We waited forever.

"Let's go," I said, "nobody home."

Right then the door opened and I had a heart attack. I swear, I had a total heart attack. I stopped breathing and I couldn't move.

Standing in front of us, dressed in a witch's costume, was the ugly woman I saw at school and at the Haunted House.

"I knew you'd come," she said.

12

I grabbed ahold of Booger's sleeve and it felt as if my arm was moving in slow motion.

"Let's go," I said.

The woman, the witch, said, "You didn't say trick or treat." Then she laughed a real witch laugh.

"Let's get out of here, Booker," I said.

"What's your hurry?" said the witch. "You didn't say trick or treat, Lizzie. You can't do anything right. I suppose you'll forget to say thank you."

"Booker," I said, "c'mon."

My voice sounded funny. It sounded slower. It almost sounded like someone else's voice.

Booger wasn't moving. He stood there staring at the witch. I didn't know if he was too afraid to move or too stupid to be afraid.

"Are you a real witch?" said Booger.

"What's real anymore?" said the witch.

Then she pointed her bony finger at me.

"Say it!" she said.

"What?" I answered. I was now pulling Booger toward the porch stairs.

The cat rubbed against my leg.

"Oh, look," she said as if she were some sweet grandmother, "he likes you."

I couldn't understand why Booger wasn't moving. It was like he was turned to stone.

"You have to say it," she said. "It's Halloween. You have to say it."

"What?" I screamed.

"Trick or treat," she said. "I have to make my choice."

"Okay, fine." I had my old voice speed back. "Trick or treat. Now we're going."

"But you don't have anything," she said. "What will it be? Trick or treat?"

"Treat," said Booger.

"Oh, don't you worry," she said, "it will be a treat."

She reached behind her and brought out a large jack-o'-lantern just crammed with candy. It was bigger and heavier than the ones we had. I thought she had to be super-strong to hold it up with one hand. She was acting as if it were as light as a balloon.

"Take as much as you want," said the witch. "There's more where this came from. I also have gingerbread children inside, if you'd like one of those. They're my favorite."

"Booker, just take one and let's get going. We've got to get home. Dad's waiting. He's probably calling the police to come get us right now," I said.

The witch laughed. I moved closer so I could see which candy he got so my parents could really check it out when we got home.

"I want lots," said Booger.

He opened his bag like he was going to shovel the candy in. He reached for the jack-o'-lantern.

The witch looked at me and said, "They were originally turnips. Pumpkins are much nicer though, don't you think?"

Something in me wanted to scream. Maybe it was the way the witch was licking her lips. I'm not sure.

I yelled, "Don't, Booker, don't touch it."

I grabbed for his arm but it was too late. He touched the jack-o'-lantern full of candy and vanished before my eyes.

The witch howled with laughter.

She said, "I love it when that happens."

"Give him back," I said.

"Not so fast," said the witch. "I gave you what you wanted. Consider it my treat."

"What do you mean?" I demanded. "I'm calling the police."

She chanted,

"Lizzie, Lizzie, had a brother, made her dizzy. He touched the jack-o'-lantern, that's too bad. Now he's the brother Lizzie had."

I started crying. I didn't know what to do. Teachers don't teach you what to do when this kind of thing happens. My parents never told me what to do if my brother touched a witch's jack-o'-lantern and disappeared.

I thought, If I hadn't had to go trick-or-treating with him, this would've never happened.

I begged, "Please give him back."

She said, "You disgust me. You can't do anything right. Want some candy?"

13

G ive him back!" I demanded.
The witch laughed at me.

"What's your costume supposed to be?" she said.

Why did I answer her? I didn't want to. I had the feeling she already knew the answer.

"I'm Elizabeth the First, Queen of England," I said.

"Oh, that's a hoot," she said. "Couldn't you make a better crown? It doesn't look like a crown. Is it supposed to be a crown? Don't you think you have on too much makeup? Don't you think you could've tried harder? Don't you think you should've been Lizzie Borden?"

When she talked, I felt as if I were being hypnotized. I was going to sleep. I felt as if I were sinking deep into mud. I was feeling as if I couldn't move. I was turning into Lizzie the Statue.

"Yes," I said slowly, "I mean, no." I shook myself. "I don't know. Leave me alone."

I tried to ignore her. I forced myself to turn around and I started down her porch steps.

"Don't listen to her," I said to myself. "She doesn't know anything."

"Just where do you think you're going?" she said.

"To get my dad," I said.

"I don't think so," she said.

Her awful stupid cat lunged in front of me and started hissing and acting like it was going to attack me.

"Come back, Lizzie," she said.

I thought about letting the cat attack me and then using that as an excuse for running away, but I chickened out and turned around and went back up on the porch.

She was faking as if she were nice again. "Lizzie, sweetums, I thought you didn't want your stupid little wittle brother around?"

"I didn't," I said, "but I didn't want him dead either."

She was back to mean. "Who says he's dead, you stupid idiot girl."

"Then where is he?" I asked.

"He's being taken care of and . . . very well . . . if you know what I mean," she said.

I didn't like the way she said that.

"I'm sorry we came here. I'm sorry for whatever we've done. I just need my little brother back and I want to go home."

67

"There's no place like home. There's no place like home. I've heard that crap before," she said. "The next thing you know, you'll want some ruby slippers."

I just stood there and cried. All my "too much makeup" was running down my face.

"Stop it," she said, "or I'll give you something to cry about. Shall I tell you what you are? Shall I tell you?"

"No," I blubbered.

She said softly, "You're a spoiled brat who only thinks of herself. Isn't that right?"

I didn't know what I was supposed to say. Was I supposed to agree with her? I didn't know what to do.

She said sharply, "You think you really want him back?"

"Yes," I said.

"Yes, what?" she said.

"Yes, please," I said.

"You don't even know how to talk right," she said. "How are you supposed to take care of a little brother you don't even want?"

"I don't know," I said, still crying.

She smiled at me.

"Let's see," she said, "let's just see if you have it in you to get him back. Wouldn't that be fun?"

"What?" I said.

"Let's just say you'll have to prove yourself. You'll have to find him. It won't be easy. Are you up for it? Or are you too scared? Too much of a crybaby?"

Before I could say yes or no, well, all I can tell you is that I saw her jack-o'-lantern flying through the air at me. I tried to duck but I think it hit me. I'm not sure, but I think it knocked me out.

14

I woke up lying on a big flat rock with clouds all around it, not fog, but clouds, fluffy clouds. There was a slight parting of the clouds and I could see the moon. Then I looked down. I had a heart attack.

I was up very high. As far as I could tell and as sure as I could be with only moonlight to see with, I was above the earth. I was in the sky on a rock.

Ahead of me was a huge, huge dark house. The rocks formed a path to it. I could clearly see when the clouds moved that the house was floating. There was nothing underneath. Then the stone underneath me moved.

Oh no, I thought, I'm sky surfing on a rock.

So how can I tell you how it feels to realize you are sitting on a floating rock that is part of a rock path leading to a floating, massively scary mansion. Crazy! That's how it feels — completely nutso, loony, batty, whatever you want to call it, but crazy.

The rocks were kind of bobbing up and down like they were floating on water. I couldn't help but wonder what was holding them up. I wondered what would happen if I just stayed there. Maybe someone in a helicopter would see me one day, or a hang glider, or someone sky jumping.

"Hi," I'd say.

"What are you doing up here?" they'd say.

"Well, it happened on Halloween," I'd say.

"Is that a floating rock?" they'd ask.

"Seems to be," I'd say.

I'd ask them to send help, but by the time they got back I would've floated away. I'd have been lost in some clouds. At least I had my Halloween candy to keep me alive. I felt around me to retrieve it.

"I don't believe it,'" I said. "She took my candy. Of all the mean rotten tricks."

I stood up. I decided that if I had to spend the rest of my life floating, I'd do it closer to the house, maybe on the porch. I stepped on the next rock.

"Help," I said weakly, as the rock went down just a little when I stepped on it.

I decided to move faster.

"It's like stepping-stones," I told myself, "if you keep moving steadily you're fine."

It was a total lie to myself. I made it up and it worked. Before I knew it I was on the porch.

"Man, this is a big house," I said, "a really big house. There must be a hundred rooms. Who am I talking to? I'm talking to myself."

Then I remembered Booger.

"Booger," I yelled, "are you in there?"

I didn't hear anything. I went over and looked through a window. I did think about dying if someone had looked back out at me. I couldn't see anything, though. It was too dark.

When I stood back from the window I noticed that the double front doors were open, wide-open.

"Yikes, they weren't open before," I said and I started breathing real fast and shallow. I was panting.

I'm turning into a dog, I thought, get ahold of yourself, Lizzie.

I took a deep breath, held it to the count of eight and let it out very slowly. I learned how to do that from watching yoga on TV. It's supposed to calm you down.

I pretended it worked. I looked in the doorway.

"Hello," I said softly, "anyone home? Trick or treat? Booger is that you?"

There was no answer. There were lights coming on though, slowly. They were weak-looking lights, very faint. It was like the whole place was on dimmers and they were being turned up. The hall lights came on first and even some candles lit themselves.

A big beautiful chandelier above the stairway

slowly came on and then eventually got a little brighter. It was almost, well sort of friendly; it was like the house was inviting me in.

I thought, Maybe they're like voice-activated or else . . . it's really haunted.

I carefully walked in. I wiped my feet first, you know, just in case. As I stepped into the hallway and started looking around, the front doors behind me slammed shut. I turned and ran toward them and I could hear them being bolted from the outside.

I turned with my back against the doors to hear the screams and laughter of something bad. The sound was moving through the house like a light wind, faint and always moving.

"Okay," I said, "I'm scared enough. Let's go home."

15

The house was almost pretty, I mean, if it was daylight and there were people around and I wasn't scared half out of my mind. From where I was standing I could see a bunch of red carpeting and a lot of big plants around. There were spears and stuff on the walls and like a coat of armor standing in the corner.

It sort of smelled funny. It smelled like our house smells when we get back from vacation and open the door. It smelled as if it needed to have the windows opened.

All the furniture looked like antiques. The place could've been a museum. It was also extremely clean. There wasn't a speck of dust anywhere. It was a spiffy haunted house, if it really was a haunted house and it was.

I only wished the lighting were a little brighter. The lights seemed as if they were on but they were antique, too, and dim. There were way too many dark corners and it was way too shadowy.

After the combination laughter and scream, the place was dead quiet. That freaked me out. I felt like I couldn't breathe or something would hear me.

I accidentally saw myself in a mirror and did the best standing broad jump of my life.

"Get a grip, Lizzie," I told myself.

I moved from the doorway, through the small hallway, and into the large room with the gigantic stairway coming down into it with the chandelier hanging above it. I could see up the stairs to what looked like a faint light coming out of a hallway. In this main room, it seemed like there were a lot of large paintings on the wall.

I went over and looked at one up close.

"Yikes," I said out loud.

It was the ugliest thing I think I'd ever seen. Well, the witch came close. However, I think this was uglier.

It was a picture of a woman with snakes coming out of her head — talk about having a bad hair day. Instead of hair, she had these live wicked-looking snakes. Her eyes looked like they were bloodshot clear into the pupil. If you ask me, she also had way too much makeup on. She was nasty-looking.

I looked down at the bottom of the picture and it said on a little plaque, MEDUSA.

I thought, Medusa, Medusa, who is Medusa?

Then I remembered. We studied her in Greek

mythology. She used to be pretty and had great hair but then she acted so snooty about it that one of the goddesses turned her into a snakehead. She then could turn people to stone if they looked her in the eye. A guy named Perseus used his shield as a mirror so he wouldn't have to look at her and cut her head off. Good-bye Medusa.

Then I saw something out of the corner of my eye. I whipped around.

"Who's there?" I said.

I grabbed a candlestick with a burning candle in it. I figured I could hit something hard enough to slow it down. I couldn't see anything. I told myself if I ever got out of there I was taking karate lessons.

I moved around the room a little, still carrying the candlestick. I was getting a little freaked out because the eyes in the Medusa painting kept following me wherever I went. I also kept seeing something move out of the corner of my eye, but when I'd turn in that direction, nothing would be there.

"I'm just jumpy," I told myself. "Big, old floating haunted houses always have things that seem scary."

I wondered if I should go upstairs.

"Do not go upstairs," I said, "stay right where you are."

A blast of air came from somewhere and blew

my candle out. It scared me and I dropped the candlestick. Then something moved again.

I turned and looked. I couldn't see anything but my shadow on the wall. Then it moved. All by itself. It got bigger and bigger and waved both of its, my arms, at me as if it were trying to get my attention.

I'm not stupid. I ran.

"Mom!" I squeaked and I ran right up those stairs.

I ran into a hallway and took a right into the first door there was. I could make out bookshelves by the moonlight coming in through the window. I thought it must be a library. I shut the door behind me.

The room was big. The moonlight was making everything look too scary. I needed some light. I tried to find a light switch. I felt along the wall.

I thought, If a hand touches me, I'm toast.

I swear to you, at that instant I felt a hand touch mine.

To say I screamed my lungs out is to put it mildly. I thought I'd screamed so hard my hair was going to fall out. I grabbed and pulled on the door handle until I could get back out in the hallway. I slammed the door shut.

What if there is someone in there and they're going to try to get me? I thought. What if I can hear them?

I could. I could hear someone running their hands across the door. They were trying to find the handle. Then the handle started to move.

I didn't wait to see who it was. I ran down the hall. I took a left and there was another hallway.

"What if it's like a maze?" I said.

It was. Every door I tried opened to another hallway. I ran and tried door after door. I ran for what seemed like an hour.

I was out of breath so I stopped to cry. I looked down both ends of the hallway. There was nothing. I was trapped and lost.

I leaned against the wall and there was my shadow looking back at me.

"Go ahead and get me," I said.

It didn't move.

"Go ahead," I yelled at it.

Very slowly it moved its hand.

I thought, This is it. It's going to hit me. I lost Booger and now a shadow is going to get me.

It didn't hit me. It took its finger and wrote on the wall. It made, I guess, shadow letters on the wall. It finished writing and slid to the floor.

The letters were fading but I could read them. They said, "Friend. Will help you."

16

My shadow wrote another message. "You're making the scary stuff."

"What do you mean?" I said. "Great, just great, it's all my fault? Everything is my fault? Thanks."

My shadow wrote, "Upstairs your scary ideas are coming true."

"What?" I said. "Because I'm afraid of something it happens? I don't get it."

It wrote, "Think up something scary."

"No way," I said.

The shadow shrugged its shoulders.

"Okay," I said, "like I have a choice. What if there was a mummy chasing me down the hall?"

Right then I heard this horrible grunting noise coming from around the corner.

I screamed, "It's a mummy! Run for your lives."

I started to run, but I could tell by the sound of its breathing it was closing on me fast. I looked over my shoulder, I could see him clearly and I noticed something strange.

The mummy was wrapped in toilet paper. Then you know what happened? The minute I thought about that toilet paper, for a second there I thought it was funny and in that second the mummy turned around and went the other way.

"Cool," I said. "All I have to do is not get scared or imagine anything scary like . . ." and my brain started thinking about vampire bats.

I stopped myself. I thought about horses instead. I was feeling pretty confident. I shouldn't have.

A door opened and the witch came out.

"Think you're smart, don't you?" she said. "Think you have it figured out?"

"Yes, I mean, no," I said.

She confuses me so bad when she talks to me. I feel like I can't think for myself.

"I suppose you think you should have your little brother back now?" she said.

"Yes," I said.

"Yes, what?" she said. "Who taught you to talk? You're so impolite."

"Yes, please," I said.

I felt myself slowing down. I felt so tired.

"Well, Lizzie, you've got some work to do, first." She laughed. Then she said very meanly, I mean, the meanest ever, "Get to the kitchen and get the dishes done, and don't you dare break one little dish. Not a one."

"Will you give my brother back then?" I asked.

"We'll see, miss little spoiled brat. We'll see."

My shadow was behind her and had its thumbs in its ears and was waving its fingers at the witch. I couldn't help it. It made me laugh.

"What's so funny?" she said.

"I wasn't laughing," I lied.

"Maybe you don't take this seriously, Lizzie. Maybe you don't take anything seriously. Maybe that's your problem. You don't care about anything."

I felt like lead.

"Sorry," I said.

"Get to work," she said.

"Where's the kitchen?" I asked.

"Now that's the first smart question you've asked," she said.

She went through another door and slammed it shut.

I gave it a couple of minutes and tried the door thinking it was probably the way to the kitchen. It was now locked.

"Great," I said.

17

"Now how am I going to find my way to the kitchen?" I asked.

My shadow pointed down the hall. I followed its directions and when I got to the end of the hallway we were in, it pointed down another hall. I went down it.

Then it pointed to a door. I opened it and went down another hall and I was at the head of the main stairway with the chandelier. Down the stairs I could see Medusa looking up at me.

I knew kitchens are always on the first floor. Right? The back door is usually to the kitchen.

I was going to slide down the banister but I didn't know what my dress would do. I walked down the stairs. I tried not to look down where that painting of Medusa was.

In the great big room my shadow extended its arm as if to say, "Right this way," and then it ran for a door at the far side of the room.

I was almost having fun following my shadow. We went through a door into a dining room, a huge dining room, with a table all set for dinner. Then we went through a swinging door and we were in the kitchen.

It was major shock time. When she said dirty dishes, she meant dirty dishes. There was every dish on the planet in this room and they were stacked a mile high and they were dirty. I mean scuz city. I bet those dishes had never been washed.

"I can't do this," I said.

I said it again, "I can't do this. I can't do this many dishes. It will take me all year."

It was also so dang hot in there you wouldn't believe it. It was sauna city. There was a fireplace in the kitchen and it had a bonfire in it. I've never seen such a big fire.

"I'm going to have a heat stroke," I said.

I tried to open the window but it wouldn't open. I stood there and took it all in for a minute. I didn't know what to do.

I didn't have a clue to what would happen if I just didn't do them. I wondered if I'd be stuck in this stupid house forever, with that witch, who had Booger hidden someplace.

I can at least try, I thought.

I found an apron and put it on. It pulled off my crown while I was putting the strap over my head. I left it off. I'm not sure why I put on an apron.

I never wear aprons. It seemed like the thing you do if you have to do a million dishes.

I next poured a bunch of soap in the sink and filled it up with warm water. I could've used cold because it would be hot in ten minutes in that room. Then I had this brilliant idea. What if I closed my eyes and thought about them all being done? Then maybe they'd all be done when I opened my eyes.

I tried it. I closed my eyes and thought about the dishes all being done. I even said a magic word to get the process going. I said, "Booga Booga."

All right, I admit it isn't the best magic word. It was, however, the only one I could think of at the time. No one is perfect. Considering that I was totally stressed out from everything that had happened, I think it was pretty good.

I opened my eyes just ready for the dishes to be done.

I even yelled, *"Ta da!"*

Guess what? The dishes were still there and dirty as ever.

Well, I thought, it was a nice try.

I wiped the sweat and some of the makeup off my face with the dish towel, and started washing one of the shorter stacks of plates. It was at least a stack I could reach the top of without pole vaulting. I scrubbed and scrubbed each dish in the stack. There were about forty plates in just this one stack and there were stacks and stacks. They were entirely gross. They were covered in dried food that could have been stuck there by superglue. It took me forever to get them clean.

I rinsed a bunch and stacked them on the side of the sink. I was feeling pretty good about myself. I felt like maybe I could get this done. Then it was horror time.

I looked at the dishes I washed and they were dirtier than when I started. They seemed to be growing dried food on them.

Maybe I didn't get them clean before I rinsed them, I thought, but I did. I know I did.

I decided to try another stack.

"At least she could've given me rubber gloves," I said, getting a stool to reach the top of one of the other stacks of plates. I'm not kidding you, they were that high up.

I stood on the stool and carefully reached for the top plate. I thought I was doing just fine. I was being supercareful. I had the plate in my hand and then something happened.

Now, I'm not completely sure what "something" was, but somehow the stool tipped just a little and I accidentally knocked over the whole stack of plates. Really, that wasn't so bad except that the stack falling over caused the next stack to fall over and then it was like dominoes. I would say about twelve to fifteen stacks actually fell, but I wasn't keeping a close count.

The witch burst through the door.

"What have you done?" she screamed.

She was so dang witchy. I started crying.

"I told you not to break a single plate. Look at you. You can't do anything right."

She was jumping up and down.

"What do you have to say for yourself!" she demanded.

"Sorry," I said, "they were too high. There were so many. How was I supposed to reach them?"

"No excuses," she said.

"Sorry," I said again.

"You can't do anything right," she said, "there is no excuse for you."

Besides, I thought but didn't say, I didn't break a single one. I probably broke about two hundred and fifty.

18

I could feel my mind slowing down as she talked. I had to find a way to fight back. I knew I had to think of something. She was completely ticked. I wasn't sure what she would do.

I came up with what I thought was a brilliant idea. At that instant, I remembered the witch from *The Wizard of Oz*. What did Dorothy do to get rid of that witch? She threw water on her and then the witch did her "I'm melting, what a world," number. Right?

I practically jumped for joy when I saw that the sink had one of those spray nozzle things. I grabbed it and pulled it out. I aimed it at the witch.

"Don't try anything. Give me my brother or I let you have it," I said.

"Don't mess with me," she screamed.

She startled me enough that I almost dropped the nozzle. She moved toward me.

"Stop or I'll shoot," I said.

Okay, I know it was a stupid thing to say. Also, it didn't work. She didn't stop.

"That's it," I said, "you're asking for it."

I pulled the trigger and nothing happened. I had forgotten to turn the water on. The witch thought this was a great joke. She stopped for a minute and tried to die by laughing.

"You can't do anything right," she said. "You can't even spray me right. What is wrong with you?"

"Fine," I said.

I kept ahold of the trigger with one hand and with my other hand and every ounce of energy I had, I turned on the faucet. A beautiful stream of water was now spraying across the room and showering the witch.

"Melt away," I said, "see if I care."

At this point I didn't care about her at all. I didn't know how I'd find Booger or get down out of that house but I'd at least get her away from me.

I drenched her and she stood there yelling. I drenched her some more and she yelled some more. I stopped for a second to check out how the melting was doing.

Something was very wrong. She looked fine. I mean, she looked wet and ugly as anything, but she wasn't melting.

"You're not melting," I said.

"Of course not, you idiot," she said.

"I don't get it. I thought you were supposed to melt," I said.

"That was in a movie, stupid. Movies aren't real, but you're too stupid to know that, aren't you?" she said.

I glanced around for my shadow, hoping that it had some great plan, but I couldn't see it. I had no idea what the witch was going to do. I thought maybe I should be prepared for the worst.

I tried to think of plan B. I didn't have a plan B. I tried to think what witches do to you.

The only thing I could think of was that they turn you into things. I hoped she wouldn't turn me into a toad. I'd probably end up on a dissection table in some science class.

However, the witch didn't do anything to me. She hissed at me, like a snake. It was pretty disgusting looking. I mean, there was like spit coming out of her mouth and stuff.

She said, "Do you want your brother?"

I just nodded "yes" to her.

"Speak up you cowardly little worm," she said.

"Yes," I said, "you know I do." I thought I'd better add something. "Sorry about the water and the dishes."

"Well," she said, "he's in the basement where he's been all along."

19

The witch then closed her eyes and folded her arms.

I thought, Oh boy, here it comes. I'm warts.

However, she didn't zap me. She was drying herself. It was really bizarro. She looked like she had built-in hair dryers under her clothes. Her clothes puffed up like a balloon. In about ten seconds flat she was dry.

She looked at me and said, "Don't you ever try something stupid like that again."

She then disappeared. I mean, like vanished into thin air. I looked at the floor with all the broken dishes on it and eight hundred gallons of water.

I said, "I would be in so much trouble at home if this happened."

This ghost voice spoke. I'm not kidding. It was coming from the ceiling and there was no one there. It sounded a little garbled. If you talked to a turkey that could speak English, that's what it sounded like.

It said, "You are."

I would've screamed but my throat was getting sore from all of the screaming I'd done earlier. I also didn't want to let whatever-it-was hear me.

I thought, I want to go home. I wish I'd never heard of Halloween. I'll be nice to my little brother. I just want to go home.

A door creaked open in the kitchen. I stood and watched it. I tried to slowly position myself in case I had to make a run for it. However, nothing happened. The door just opened slightly and it stayed that way.

Booger is in the basement, I thought, but how can there be a basement in a floating house? Dumb question, Lizzie, how can there be a floating house?

I'm not sure why, but I had a feeling that the door that was open went to the basement. I didn't know what to do. Why would the witch tell me that truth about where Booger was? Maybe it was only a trick.

I hated it. There was only one way to find out. I had to go into the dang basement. I took off the apron. I didn't need anything to make me hotter.

What if it's a dungeon? I thought.

Every scary movie I've ever seen, people go into the basement and they are so stupid to do it.

Everyone knows that when things are scary or the lights go out, you don't go down to the basement no matter what. I scream at the actors. I yell at them every time they start to go down the stairs. I know what's in the basement.

I tell them, "You are a maniac. Do you hear me? Do not go into the basement. The killer is always in the basement. The bad people are always in the basement."

When I have my own house, it won't have a basement even near it. It will have a swimming pool and a garage with a convertible in it. It won't have a basement.

I inched my way over to the door and pushed on it with my toe. I could see it was pitch-black down there at the bottom. It was definitely a way to a basement. It had stairs and they were going down. I could feel cool air. That at least was a relief.

"Booger?" I whispered. Then I said it a little louder. "Booger, are you down there?"

I thought I heard him. He sounded far away and I could just make out what I thought were the words, "Trick or treat."

"Booger," I said, "if you're just fooling around I'm really going to let you have it. I mean it. Come up here."

I moved a little closer and looked down the stairs.

I said, "This looks familiar."

It looked very familiar. It looked sort of like our stairway at home. I looked at it some more and I realized it looked exactly like our stairway at home. I checked the top step. It was there. My name was there.

When I was real young, I wrote my name in orange crayon on the top step. Every time you went to the basement, you saw "Elizabeth" upside down.

I don't even remember getting in trouble for it. I don't even remember why I did it. I must have done it before I was afraid of the basement.

This stairway was exactly like ours at home. I mean, exactly.

"What is this?" I said.

Thank goodness no one answered.

A shiver went up my back. I was completely overwhelmed by all the scary times I'd lived through going down into our basement at home.

"I'm not going," I said to myself. "I can't. I have trouble enough at home. I can't go into the basement of a haunted house that looks like my basement at home. That's it. I've reached my limit. Sorry Booger."

I turned around and gave just a pinch of a scream. The dishes and water were gone.

20

I really need a plan bad," I told myself. "I can't go down there without a plan. How can I be sure Booger is really down there?"

I had backed away from the door until I was about six feet away.

I thought about the story of the guy that was too stupid to be afraid. That when he wasn't afraid he could think better. I also remembered that sometimes you just do things whether you're afraid or not — like going on roller coasters and stuff.

I asked myself, since there was no one else to ask, "What are you afraid of?"

I answered myself, "Give me a break, there is tons of stuff to be afraid of here. Where do you want me to start?"

I told myself to be specific about what scared me most.

"I'm afraid of something scaring me. I guess I'm afraid of being afraid."

That seemed a little weird but it made sense.

"Okay," I told myself, "if that's all I'm afraid of, I'll march right down those stairs, get Booger, and then we'll go outside and wait for a passing airplane."

I realized I was flipping out and I was getting a headache from talking to myself too much.

Why do I have to go to the basement? I thought.

I answered myself again. "Because that's where Booger is or where he's supposed to be."

"But what if he isn't?"

Finally I couldn't answer myself.

"What if it's all just a trick to keep me in this stupid house forever?"

The answer was that I'd never know until I went down there. It's like the boy who lost his money outside the house. He decided to go inside to look for it because it was much easier to look inside.

I had to look where Booger was supposed to be. I walked to the edge of the stairs. It was dark and quiet, very dark and very quiet.

I reached for the light switch for the light above the stairs. I flicked it on. The light came on and immediately I heard the light bulb make a fuzzy noise. It burnt out and the stairway was again dark.

Terrific, I thought, that means I have to go to the bottom to turn on the light there. What if it burns out, too?

I stood there a few minutes. My mind was blank. Then I heard something. It was Booger's voice again. He sounded far away and muffled.

"Lizzie, help," he said.

"I'm coming," I said, "I'm coming. Where are you?"

There was no answer.

"Go, Lizzie, go," I said to myself.

I stepped on the first step and then stepped back. I was like a tap dancer in a movie. I then tried it again. This time I went down two and stood there. My weight shifting back and forth was making the stair creak.

I moved to the next one to make it stop. It didn't and now I was more in the dark than ever. Of course you know what happened next. The door behind me slammed shut and I had my two hundredth heart attack.

I was trapped in the basement and I screamed like anything. It didn't do any good. In fact, it scared me more.

I was turning around to go back up the stairs when I heard the door bolt and lock. I heard all kinds of footsteps above me. It sounded like the room was full of people or monsters or zombies or vampires.

I had no choice. I hate having no choice. I had to go deeper into the basement. The only other choice was, I guess, to stay where I was until someone found me, but was that a choice? I inched my way down the stairs. I was going to put my hands on the wall to support me but I didn't. I didn't want to accidentally touch anything or have it touch me.

"I'm not going to be afraid," I said, but my legs were shaking and I had a lump in my throat and my stomach was doing gymnastics.

I stepped down and then down again. I kept going. I went a long, long way. I started counting the steps. I quit at one hundred and fifty-eight. I hadn't reached the bottom.

"This is ridiculous," I said, "how far down is this basement?"

Then because it was dark and I was exhausted, I momentarily lost my balance. Lucky for me I fell backward. I didn't fall very far. My back hit something round and hard.

I reached behind me and felt it. It was the door-knob to the kitchen door. I hadn't moved an inch. It was like I was on an escalator going the wrong way.

"I'll go down really fast," I thought.

Talk about dumb — I ran in the dark, down the stairs. I stopped when I was out of breath. I reached behind me.

I wanted to tear that dang doorknob off the door. I was still at the top of the steps. I hadn't moved an inch. After all that wasted energy, I was back where I started. Then I had this brilliant idea. If I ended up at the top when I tried to go down, then maybe if I tried to go up, I'd be at the bottom. I was going to face the door and try to go up. Either I would be at the bottom of the stairs or I would smash my face into the door. It was worth a try.

I turned around, put my hands in front of my face and even though I was on the top step I stepped up. I didn't hit the door. In fact I wasn't on steps anymore. I turned around carefully. I was at the bottom. I hesitated and then threw my arm out toward the light switch. I was reaching where the light switch was in our house. It was right there. I flicked it on. A lone light bulb shone in the middle of the room and I screamed — one more time.

It was my basement. I mean, it looked exactly like our basement at home and it smelled exactly like our basement at home. However, this basement had one ugly witch in the middle of the room, which our basement at home did not have and there were large orange things in the corner.

The witch said, "It's about time."

21

Welcome to the basement," said the witch. "It's exactly where you belong, isn't it? Now, let me tell you some things about yourself."

She started in telling me about everything I do wrong. I mean she was yelling at me nonstop about things that I'd totally forgotten. Things like the time I forgot to wear underwear to school and I had a dress on. I mean, I was in kindergarten. It was no big deal. The school secretary let me call my mom.

Again, the more she talked and criticized me the heavier I felt. I really felt as if I were turning to stone. The sound of her voice was making me feel as if I couldn't move. I felt like a big rock. I felt cold and thick.

Medusa, I thought, she's like Medusa and her snakes, turning people into stone by looking at them. However, she's turning me to stone with her words.

I looked down at my shoes sticking out from

underneath my dress. I know the light wasn't that good and my mental state wasn't the best, but I am willing to swear to you that my feet were actually turning into stone. It seemed as if every word she said turned a little more of me into a slab of rock. I figured at the rate she was going I'd be a statue in a matter of minutes.

I need a shield, I thought. Perseus fought Medusa with a shield. He looked into his shiny shield so he wouldn't have to look directly at her. I need a shield. What can I use for a shield? I can't think. She won't shut up.

I plugged my ears to try to think.

"That's it," I said out loud.

I had to plug my ears. I had to stop listening to the witch. If I didn't listen to her I was okay.

I left my fingers in my ears and sang. It was no particular song. I just made one up. It was very loud so I couldn't hear her.

It worked. I felt myself able to move and able to think. I looked down. I could see the toes of my shoes and they were no longer stone.

I left my fingers in and looked around the room for Booger. The witch kept yelling and I could tell she was getting louder. She was also getting madder.

I thought, It could really be toad time.

I took one finger out for a second.

"Don't you plug your ears," she said. "If you know what is good for you, which you don't. I

want to tell you about all the homework you didn't
do and all the papers you rushed and were sloppy
with. You just don't care."

It only took that much and I was feeling par-
alyzed again. I moved my fingers toward my
ears.

The witch saw me do it and screamed, "No you
don't!"

"Yes I do," I screamed back, "I don't have to
listen to you."

She ran over to me and grabbed my arms. It
felt gruesome. It was the worst. I hated her touch-
ing me. Her bony hands were cold and wet and
sticky.

"Stop it," I said and I tried to jerk away.

I heard Booger.

"Lizzie," he said.

His voice was coming from the orange things.

"Lizzie," he said again.

I was now doing professional wrestling with the
dang witch. I hate to admit it but she was beating
me. She was stronger than me, but then she made
a crucial mistake.

She wasn't watching her feet. I slammed my
foot down on top of hers and then I kicked her in
the knee. It was enough to get my right hand free.
I was going to punch her in the nose but her nose
was so big and long that mostly just from instinct
I grabbed ahold of it. Then I pulled on it. I gave
it a really good yank.

Her nose came off. I mean, not just her nose but her whole head and actually her body, too. It all came off like a one-piece costume.

I looked at my hand in a state of shock. Then I looked at the witch not knowing what to expect. I felt hot and weird and I thought I was going to puke.

Standing in front of me was — me! I was looking at myself. It was me but it was me dressed as a beautiful fairy-tale queen with a beautiful jeweled crown. I stared at myself and my queen self smiled back at me and then she slowly faded till there was nothing there.

"Help, Lizzie," Booger said.

I went over to the orange things.

"Wow," I said, "they're giant pumpkins."

They were huge. They were the biggest pumpkins you could ever find. You would win so many prizes for these pumpkins if you grew them. You would be in every record book there is.

"Booger?" I shouted.

"I'm in here," he said. "Get me out."

"Where in here?" I said.

"In the pumpkin," he said.

"Which one?" I said. "There must be a hundred of them."

"A big one," he yelled.

"Oh, *that* helps," I said, "they're all big. Keep talking. I'll find you. Sing something."

"What should I sing?" he asked.

"How should I know?" I said, climbing over each pumpkin and putting my ear next to it.

The idiot started singing "Jingle Bells." He was louder so I knew I was getting closer.

"Booger, it is Halloween, not Christmas," I screamed.

"It's the only thing I could think of," he said.

I could hear him pretty good. Then I realized I was on top of him. I was on top of the pumpkin he was in.

"I found you," I screamed. "You're in here!"

"Get me out!" he yelled.

"Say pretty please with sugar on top," I said.

He started crying.

"I'm just kidding," I said.

Then I wondered how I was going to get him out.

There was an ax leaning against the wall.

"Look out," I said. "Get to the back. I'm going to chop you out."

"Be careful," said Booger.

"Now don't start telling me what to do," I said. "Do you want out or not?"

He didn't answer.

I lifted the ax and took a swing at the pumpkin. As the blade hit the pumpkin both the pumpkin and the ax became like light molecules, like insects made of light, which flew out in a million directions. Nothing was left but Booger.

"Booger," I yelled and I hugged him. I really had missed him — and not just because I would've been in trouble if I'd come home without him. I'd missed him. Call me crazy.

22

L et's get out of here," I said.

"Where are we?" said Booker, "and where's my candy?"

"Don't push it, Booker. We're in a haunted house and I don't know how we'll get out."

"We're in our basement," he said, "how did we get here? Where is my candy?"

"The witch put you here. She put you inside a pumpkin," I said.

"A witch?" he said. "Why are we in our basement?"

"You stupid idiot," I started to say but didn't. "Booker, it just looks like our basement. We have to get out."

"I'm going upstairs," he said.

"The door is locked," I said.

"It isn't either," he said, marching up the stairs.

He turned the knob and opened the door. There was my dad. He was standing in our kitchen.

"What kind of trick are you two trying to pull?"

he asked. "Were you going to scare me with spooky sounds from the basement?"

"Dad," I screamed and ran up the stairs.

"I lost my candy," said Booker, "or Lizzie lost it."

"I didn't either," I said.

"Here it is," said my dad. "The doorbell rang and no one was there but your sacks of candy. I figured you were playing a trick on me."

I looked at him very confused. "This is really our house?" I asked.

"Was last time I looked," he said.

Booker was now busy eating some of his candy.

"Come on you two," said my dad, "we'll be late for the carnival."

"What?" I said.

"C'mon," he said and headed for the front door.

"Okay," I said weakly and followed him.

I glanced in the mirror by our front door. I looked horrible. I looked like I'd been through a war and a half. I'd lost my crown. My makeup was only a dirty outline at the very edges of my face.

"Great costume, Lizzie. Can't you do anything right?" I said but caught myself. I sounded like someone I didn't want to sound like. "You look fine," I said instead.

We went to the carnival. Guess who was the first person I saw. It was Scott.

He took one look at me and said, "Who are you supposed to be?"

"Queen Elizabeth," I said.

He said, "You don't look like a queen."

I knew I didn't. I didn't know what I looked like. Then something popped into my head.

I said, "I am too a Queen. I'm Queen Lizzie Borden the First."

"Cool," he said.

"Lizzie," my mom said when she saw my face, "what happened?"

"The witch got me, Mom," I said.

She hugged me.

"You're such a tricker," she said. "Booker told me he's never had so much fun trick-or-treating."

"Mom," I said, "I'm not kidding."

"Oh, Lizzie," she said, "get some popcorn and have some fun."

She went over to the cakewalk where someone had accidentally sat on one of the cakes. I felt someone tapping my shoulder. I turned around. There wasn't anyone there. Then something caught my eye. There was a shadow on the wall waving to me and pointing to one of the decorations. It was a witch sitting on a huge pumpkin. She was holding a sign that said HAPPY HALLOWEEN.

"Trick or treat," I said.